Gone Too Soon

Gone Too Soon

BY

NAVIMAYR LOPEZ

AuthorHouse™ LLC
1663 Liberty Drive
Bloomington, IN 47403
www.authorhouse.com
Phone: 1-800-839-8640

Published by AuthorHouse   07/20/2013

ISBN: 978-1-4817-7799-5 (sc)
ISBN: 978-1-4817-7798-8 (e)

Library of Congress Control Number: 2013912906

Contents

Dedication

I would like to dedicate this book to so many supportive people in my life. For starters, my Creative Writing teacher, Miss Thompson, who gave her creative writing class, the project of creating an original storybook and so many other fun projects that dealt with making up fun stories. The next people I'd like to thank and recognize are not just any people, but my dear, loving parents who support me all the way in whatever I do. Thanks so much for making this dream come true for me. I would like to thank my many fans who are basically called friends, for supporting me in this new chapter of my book in life. And last but not least, and yet first in my life, to God, the One who has stood by me through thick and thin and able to allow me this opportunity to share my skills with the world, thank you!

For the new readers of my book out there, I believe with all my heart, you did not make a mistake in choosing to read this book. I am super happy you have chosen this book for a fun-loving, short summer reading because you won't regret it. Thank you!

Chapter 1

"Graduating class of 2000, and majoring in crime scene investigation, Lance Marshall." Lance Marshall's friends cheered loudly and managed for the restricted bullhorn to strike the air. Everyone applauded. The end was coming to a close and when the president of the University of Illinois said "Congratulations," Lance and every one of his college classmates snapped up their caps and flung them in the air. The ceremony ended and Lance gathered with his buddies outside. Lance had applied for the University of Illinois and had received his bachelor's degree. He moved there as soon as he was certified as a college student.

His mother had wanted nothing to do with him when he had been born for reasons he still didn't know why. He always thought that maybe the reason his mother didn't want him was because his father had never come to his birth and she feared of raising a child on her own. But she wasn't really alone. She had his Grammy. At least his mother was wise enough to leave him at his Grammy Evelyn's house, and that's when she left. He was Grammy's business from then on.

Grammy Evelyn was the best thing that ever happened to him. He thanked God everyday for the miracle He put in Lance's life. Lance was with his Grammy ever since his first week of life, and he couldn't imagine not having her in his life. She was his guardian angel! She had changed his diapers, taught him how to drive, and especially how to treat a girl (good or bad). "Speaking of bad girls right now," thought Lance.

"Lance! Hi! Uh . . . I just wanted to say how proud I am of you. You're going to do great. Do you wanna grab a drink or something?" her name was Linette. She wasn't a 'bad' girl, but she just tried to get what she wanted. Guys usually went for that kind of stuff, but that certainly wasn't Lance. She always tried to find ways for Lance to make a move on her and when Lance did no such thing she'd decided to be the one to plant a smooch on him. That was when Lance had the last straw, and left in storms piling up in his head. This girl was insane! He didn't want her!

She tried to hug him, but Lance didn't let her. Of course he wasn't physical with her because that was no way to treat a lady, but he wasn't going to stand around and wait for those baloney lips to land on him. No sirreee! He was going to lay down the line once and for all. "Linette! Stop this nonsense. I am not foolish, and I hope you understand when I say I want nothing to do with you. You are not the type of girl

I'm interested in. Besides, I'm taken." He didn't want to lie, but a man's gotta do what a man's got to do!

"What's her name?" asked Linette taken aback, but tried not to let it affect her. "Her name is Evelyn," lied Lance. 'Yeah, Lance the Liar. Good start to his reputation', thought Lance. 'And so far they're going to love that he's dating his grandmother. Ha! He'll get a kick out of that later on.'

"Well, she's a very lucky girl," said Linette stridently. She forced a smile on her lips, and turned on her heels to leave. Lance stood wide eyed as he thought of how he could have just said that when he first met her. His buddies who watched the whole thing finally walked up to him and they all patted his back and laughed at how well he handled the situation. His best friend Richard whom he first bunked with his first year there invited him to the party. "Lance. Why don't you follow me to the party? It'll be awesome checking out the ladies! Haha . . ."

"I don't know. I uh really just wanted to-," replied Lance before Richard cut him off. "Aww come on Lance. This should be the best night of your life! Enjoy it will you?"

"Alright, haha. I'll be right behind you," said Lance a little defeated. He hopped on in his truck, started the engine and drove off, trailing behind his pal. His truck barely had enough room to "breathe" on the same street as the party. So many cars were lined against both sides of the tiny drive way. He parked a little farther away; that meant he'd have to walk a little distance. He didn't want to risk the possibility of cops intruding or tow trucks pulling or something ridiculous. He had some good running skills so in any case he could just run his way back to his truck.

The noise blasted his ears once he reached the inside. 'This is crazy,' thought Lance. 'I should be home relaxing; talking to Grammy. Grammy,' he thought. 'The love of his life.' He smiled at the thought. It was like a club in there, people dancing tight against each other, drinks in every corner, everything out of order. This was so unlike Lance to even be in there. 'What the heck are you doing Lance?' He didn't even want to be there, and he knew it. What would he gain from this? A bad headache maybe? The music got louder by the second and added more stress to his already pounding eardrums. He never had a passion for rock or hip hop music. His kind was more of the soft jazz, punk jazz, classical jazz . . . basically anything jazz, really.

He couldn't find Richard from the moment he got there. He decided to leave and tell Richard in the morning. As he started out the door a slender hand yanked him by his biceps and pulled him towards a red headed, little drunk, pretty female. A chick he never encountered before was trying to get it on . . . with him! How despicable. "No!" he yelled through the deafening racket. He pulled her away from him and felt a vibration coming from his back left pocket. It was his phone.

His cousin Leila was calling him; she had already called him twice, and he missed both her calls. He tugged away from the drunken girl and stepped outside. People kept plunging in the house through the door making the already crowded house packed! "Leila?" he answered. "Lance you have to come quick! It's Grammy Evelyn!" Leila blabbered and panicked on the phone.

"What? Wait a minute . . . what's wrong? Leila, Leila! Slow down . . . Tell me what's going on . . . What is it?" said Lance trying to soothe his freaked out cousin. She continued to rush into what was wrong with his grandmother as she sobbed. However, Lance hadn't anticipated the next thing she said. Everything around him stopped. The Earth beneath him froze. He felt his shoulders start to sag down by the minute. He stood heavily, bearing the realization of what his cousin was saying, of what was wrong with his Grammy, of what might happen if he lost his guardian angel.

Chapter 2

Everything was dark except for the lamp on the night dresser. He sat on the edge of his bed with his phone placed nestled next to his ear. His elbows rested on his knees and his anguished expression faced the wall. Lance listened to Leila, now much calmer; explain about Grammy Evelyn's condition. He rubbed his forehead right to left with his hand.

"Her heart is in an unstable condition and the doctors considered surgery like uh . . . They called it something like a triple bypass, but one of the experts there thought her heart might be too weak for the procedure. They say it can come close to heart failure, but aren't so sure. She's stable at the moment, but Lance . . . you have to come. All Grammy has is us," said Leila.

"Leila, of course I'll go! I had a job interview in two days, but I don't care when it comes to family. I'll cancel it and board a plane tomorrow morning. I'll rest in the plane and then be in time for lunch with my wonderful cuz," replied Lance.

"Oh so you'll take a cab when your plane arrives?" asked Leila.

"No silly! You're picking me up. Just ask one of the better nurses to stay with Grammy. It'll be fun Leila; some one-on-one time with my cousin."

"Well you get down to business quick! Haha wow Lance. Alright I'll come get you. I know it'll hurt, but I'll just have to endure the pain!" said Leila.

"Family first right? Thanks cuz. I'll call you before I leave and then when I get off the plane. Can't wait to see you either . . . . Yea . . . okay . . . alright! Bye, love you too," Lance ended off in a smile. He was happy he had someone to rely on other than Grammy.

Lance grabbed some of his warmer clothes; he had to brace himself for the chillness of Pagosa Springs, Colorado. He got everything ready ahead of time so he could change, grab some coffee, and go. Lance got ready for bed as soon as he finished his packing. He lay down in his bed, and thought about the events to come. He played everything out in his mind and hoped the best part was that Grammy Evelyn would come out great and healthy.

Next morning, Lance awoke to his alarm clock, pushing it aside and heading towards the bathroom. He decided to shower first to feel fresh and ready. He shaved, gelled his hair, and dressed in a thermal long sleeve shirt, jeans, and to top it all off, his black leather jacket. Grabbing his coffee, he headed towards the airport in a taxi to leave Illinois.

After going through the screening process, he sat down at his gate to finish putting a sneaker on. His phone buzzed in his pocket again and it was Richard. "Where were you last night? Could not find you!" Lance smirked at the message and was sending his reply when someone walked past him and dropped their book.

Chapter 3

He glanced up at the person who had dropped their belongings. It was a she and 'she' kept on walking. Lance picked it up and looked at the cover. It was a suspenseful book called "Crime Uncovered". He had read that book once or twice; he really enjoyed it because he was a reader, and he loved all the mystery. Plus, becoming a crime scene investigator, he needed some tips and pointers and so he eventually caught on to a few mentioned in the book.

He looked to find the 'she' that lost it. He had only seen her back and saw what she was wearing. She had a purple beanie with long black bouncy curls down at her back, and she wore a skirt with black leggings and black ankle boots. "My kind of style," he thought; he then pushed it aside. He was here to board a plane and get to his destination, not be enchanted by a woman (whom he hadn't even met yet).

He spotted her at a Starbucks bar waiting for her order. She was still to her back when he called out to her. "Um . . . Hey, miss! You dropped your book." Suddenly she turned around and he looked up from the book to the most gorgeous sight he ever saw. Lance was in a trance. He felt his jaw sort of drop down! From his point of view he saw how her windblown hair fluttered in the air and showed off her perfect diamond shaped head. Her rosy cheeks made his heart warm, although he didn't know why. His coffee gave off warmth, but he didn't feel the same way as when he watched her. "I uh . . . hehe, you uh . . ." Lance choked up as he tried to find his words. "Ahem, you dropped your book." He smiled at her, finally being able to speak. Her lips parted into a grin.

"Oh! Thank you. I didn't feel it drop. You're so kind. Thanks again." All the while Lance was just staring at her with some googly eyes. "Dude look away!" he thought. "Oh yeah, sure! You're so very welcome." He didn't want to leave but his flight was soon to depart and he wanted to be there to settle in quick. He grinned at her but turned around swiftly back to his flights gate.

Sitting back down, he caught some eyes staring at him. The gorgeous beauty of whom he didn't get the name of, had sat down a few seats away from him, but was no longer staring at him. She popped out the book he had gracefully returned to her and began to read it. He shot an eyebrow up in bemusement, and slightly turned his head towards her. She seemed to have caught the hopeless peeking and met his gaze. Lance once more flashed his mouthful of perfect, straight teeth and finally got the courage to say what he wanted to say.

"Hey," he chuckled. "I didn't quite catch your name," he said waiting patiently for a response. She bookmarked her page and extended out her delicate hand to Lance. "I'm Nancy," she politely replied.

"Nancy. Lovely name. Where you headed?" he started the conversation. He noticed her stunning eyes, the color of violet-green, stare him back in the face, her eyes fluttering open carefully with each blink. "Earth to Lance!" he shouted to his mind. He shook his head a little and she pointed to the same gate as his.

"Really? Me too! What are you going for?" he was a little excited and he didn't know why. I mean, he just met this girl and was already thinking too far ahead. He needed to keep his cool. She giggled softly under her breath. Lance felt like the soft laughter that ejected her mouth was like the best music in the world, the greatest sound on earth that made his heart leap. Wow? Could she really be doing this to him? He was starting to think he was insane. Her lips gave a heart-warming smile. They looked so soft and pretty that he just melted. This was crazy; he needed his mind on something else fast!

Luckily, she began talking, "Well . . . I'm visiting my Tia Norma. She said that we had to do something special. Now I don't really know what for, but I can't wait to see her and see what this big surprise is all about."

"Flight destination to Colorado. Boarding all classes now." Both Lance and Nancy stood and boarded the plane. Coincidently, they had been seated a row away from each other. However, Lance had felt them click instantly and didn't want to give it away so fast. So he asked an elderly woman if he could switch spots with her. The sweet old lady agreed immediately, and so that put Lance and Nancy right beside each other. They made themselves comfortable, while Lance pulled out his cell phone to make a call to Leila to tell her he was on his way.

The flight soon made its way to depart, and the two of them began chatting instantly. "Why are you headed to Colorado, Lance?" asked Nancy. She had taken off her beanie, and put it away to allow the lovely honey scented shampoo drift to his nose. He breathed in the aroma and spoke, "I recently graduated college . . . a few days ago actually, and I'm very happy because I was looking forward to my job interview for the Illinois police department to become a crime scene investigator after all the police training stuff. Anyways, I got a call from my cousin Leila and she told me that . . . she told me that the most important person in my life is sick, really sick. And I have to be there with her."

Nancy's eyes grew wide as she felt the compassion coming out of his voice. She listened with an open ear and he felt as if he could drain himself out to her. Even though they had just met he had felt a minimal bond. Yeah it might be tiny, but there was still a bond. He suddenly grew an urge to kiss her lips, but thought wrong of it to do it so fast without getting to know her well; well, at all in his case. However trying to stop himself, he couldn't and his body leaned in to the attractiveness of her lips. He was met with a fiery hand slap on the face. If he thought he could get her so easily, he was wrong.

Nancy surprised at his behavior saw what he was about to do and unwelcomed his vulnerability. She leaned far back in her seat away from Lance and looked at him with even wider eyes than before, only this time they weren't of sorrow, but of anger. "How could you do this Lance?! What are you insane? I don't even know you that well!" she established. Lance took a deep breath of air and blinked his eyes a few times. He then tried to calm Nancy down, "Shh! Nancy, Nancy . . . I'm sorry; just lower your voice down."

"You have a girlfriend and you're supposed to be there with *her*," she whispered. "Don't you have any respect? Any humanity? Lance we hit it off so well and now you're throwing it all away. I know we just met, but you made me think you were different than other guys. But then again you also have a girlfriend, so I don't know what to think."

"No Nancy you don't understand. The most important person in my life is—" started Lance, but was cut off by Nancy who wouldn't have any of it.

"No Lance. *You* don't understand! I'm getting the security on board to come and get you because I can't stand to be with a person who is a liar *and* a cheater. Been there, done that. And certainly not interested." The security on board came and took Lance because Nancy reported that he was a threat to her so they tied his hands with the hard plastic cuffs.

Chapter 4

"Ouch," said the security guard. "Looks like you got yourself a problem. Want to tell me about it?" offered the guard. "Hey look man, my names Ralph. Been on this plane thousands of times with so many different cases, but yours is certainly my first I've dealt with . . . so who is she? Your girlfriend? Your lover? Some secret admirer? Haha . . ." he laughed at his suggestions.

"What? No man! I just met her . . ." replied Lance with a sigh.

"Whoa! Not cool man! Not cool. Now I understand why she's upset. You know man, wait what's your name?" said Ralph with his long beard and crinkly brown hair.

"Look, I know what you're going to say. I'm a player, I'm an idiot . . . I don't know! Whatever you want, but listen I'm not that kind of guy! My grandmother always told me to treat a woman like a princess. She's a flower you know? You got to know the right amount of water to pour, the right amount of sunlight to let shine, the right amount of nutrients, the right amount of everything, so that when that flower blossoms, she'll bloom into the best rose of the bunch . . . and by the way, my name's Lance, Ralph."

All the while, Ralph was looking at Lance mesmerized at what he said. Ralph rested his elbow on one arm with his hand rubbing his chin. His mouth was slightly open taking in what Lance was saying. "Wow . . . then why did you make a move on her?" crackled Ralph. His burst of laughter was abrupt and caught Lance by surprise. Lance sighed and thought about Ralph's question. Lance knew he made the wrong move, but was taught to love a girl the right way. He wondered if he'd ever get his chance with that girl, Nancy. He sighed again.

"Well, I really need to apologize to her. I'm really not who you thought I was back there. I really know that when a girl's hurt, she needs a shoulder to cry on, and when she smiles you make her laugh," said Lance trying to get Ralph on his side. Ralph had settled down and leaned back in his seat bringing his arms behind his head as a cushion. He popped an eyebrow up as if to make sure Lance was telling the truth.

"You know, Lance. I have heard that so many times from the guys that do that! They are such losers! And you too! But! You sound sincere and down to earth, and the eyes . . . the eyes they tell a story and your eyes . . . well they are telling the truth," said Ralph. Lance a little surprised at Ralph's message looked at him with squinted eyes and a smirk. Ralph smiled and nodded his head slightly, then he took a deep breath and dozed off.

The plane's wheels hit the floor and the plane did a bounce. Lance jumped in his seat from his nap. He realized they had arrived at Colorado. He smiled. He would soon get to see his Grammy! Apparently Ralph hadn't felt anything and was still asleep. His head lay between the seat and the window, his mouth open, his nose flaring up and down with each snore. Lance needed his hands out of that hard plastic cuff band. People continued to board off while Ralph snoozed.

Nancy looked very upset as she passed him by, and she eyed him with a sad heart, feeling that her chance at friendship with him was a goner. Lance called to her, "Nancy!" but she didn't look back. "Ugh! Ralph, get me out of this thing!" cried Lance. He elbowed Ralph in the arm with a hard thud who yelped awake from his intoxicating sleep.

"Whoa! Ow man! What it's it to ya?!" he cried. Lance raised his cuffed hands to Ralph's face. Ralph quickly went to get scissors and cut off Lance's wrist cuffs. Lance grabbed his bag and sprinted out the airplane. Flight crew members and staff told him to slow down, but he kept on running trying to find Nancy. Nowhere to be found, he stopped and turned all the way around. He tried looking for her purple beanie or the cover of her book, but no clue as to where she was helped him out. He suddenly eyed a pair of ankle boots from behind a suitcase and raced towards it.

He was misguided and the woman who owned the pair was not close to Nancy. He breathed a sigh and his shoulders sagged down with the weight of his duffel bag. "She's amazing," he breathed out. Then he heard a familiar voice behind him say, "Who's amazing?"

Chapter 5

Lance turned around to find Leila, his cousin. "Leila! I haven't even called you yet," he smiled as he leaned in to hug his cousin. They embraced the hug for a good two minutes, and finally loosened up to look each other in the face. Leila was a very beautiful woman. Her jawline was expressed as dignified, independent, and joyful when she smiled. Her eyes sparkled in daylight or in the dark night. Her posture was slender and definite; she rarely slumped over. Her skinny frame showed that she was in good shape, and she almost never showed any signs of fear. Leila wasn't married, but the guy who'd steal her heart would be very lucky.

His cousin was a part of his mother's side too. Sadly his aunt and uncle had died in a car wreck, and Leila was a changed person after that. Instead of living freely with no rules, she knew it was never her type of life. Leila joined a Seventh-day Adventist church, got baptized, and became a member. He was happy for her; he knew she was on the right path. He thought he had been on a similar path, but now with all this going on, he just seemed lost.

"So cuz? Who's amazing?" asked Leila. "You seemed like you were searching for someone. Who?

'Cause you should've been looking for me. You know that right?" Leila crackled at her own joke. Lance eased and his shoulders let out a huge sigh. He wrapped his arm around her shoulder and squeezed her. Then as they began to walk he kissed her forehead.

"What? You leaned in to kiss her?? You're crazy Lance. Of course I would have slapped you too!" Said Leila amazed at her cousins behavior. "Didn't Grammy teach you how to treat a lady? Apparently you haven't gotten the memo," giggled Leila. They were in the car on their way to eat lunch at Olive Garden. Lance rested his elbow on the door leaning his head against it. He rolled his eyes towards the back of his head listening to Leila tease him. He was such an idiot he thought.

As they continued to drive on, Lance looked outside at all the pine-needle trees, the big snow covered mountains, the log cabins separated for miles from their neighbors. It was his kind of town. He always loved the country side areas where the grasslands stretched for miles without any disruptions and where the weather was chilly and fresh. He wondered why he had decided to pack his bags and move away from it all, the state he loved most.

As they reached the Italian restaurant, Leila parked the car and got out with Lance. Once inside, they were seated by a female waitress who then took their order for their beverages. Looking at the menus, they ordered their meals and finally conversed. "So how's Grammy coming along?" asked Lance. "Is she doing any better?" Leila stayed silent for a while. She just stared at Lance thinking of how to say their Grammy's condition.

"Well, I saw her this morning before I went to pick you up at the airport. She was wrinkly. And she was warm this time. Not cold like she has been for the past few days. It's like she knew you were coming to visit her. Her adopted son has now arrived to see his Grammy, and she knows this. A bond so strong that can't be separated even long after either one of you is gone." She stopped there. She had been speaking these details with a faint smile, just looking off in the distance with a dazed gaze in her eyes. Lance listened openly to what Leila was saying. He had a tiny smile too; just a tiny sparkle of a reminder with this feeling for the greatest person in the world.

"Warm. That's how she's always been around me," replied Lance after a while. Leila chuckled. "That's how any girl's ever felt around you Lance. Haha for goodness sake, you're a one and a million guy, and any girl, I mean *any,* is lucky to have you as their man. Please though, Lance. Don't throw it away!"

Lance laughed and looked at his darling cousin. "You know I was thinking the exact same thing about you. Any guy is lucky to have you, but he'd be crazy not to keep you for the rest of his life. And if he hurts you, you come get me. I'm serious Leila; I'll be there faster than you can even pick up the phone to call. Ok?" they laughed in mildness, giving off a good vibe from their table. They continued to smile as their meals arrived at their table.

They allowed the lightness of the conversation to go on like a flowing river. Lance would start talking about his career, and what he'd do while he was in Colorado, and sometimes hint that he wanted to find Nancy to apologize for his complete idiocy. Leila would then answer with her same obvious remarks, but continue to talk about Grammy very soothingly like she always did when she spoke about her. The two cousins were very fond of each other, and if Lance didn't know any better he would have just started calling her his sister, because that's what they had become basically; siblings.

They had grown up together way before Leila's parents had died. His aunt and uncle were compassionate with him when they saw Lance, and did love him as a son, but he never cared to live with them as much as he wanted to live with Grammy when they offered him. He'd sleep over once in a while, and sometimes went to visit in the summer for a few family vacation trips. In the end, his favorite choice was to spend his time with his Grammy, especially cuddle up with her when it was cold. They would sit on the couch together and sip hot chocolate, and she would tickle his nose with the usual Eskimo kiss and they would share many laughs. Then she'd wrap her soft, long arms around him, and kiss him to death all around his little cheeks. He'd scream and shout, but knew all the time that he loved it. He didn't care about anything, just her.

He was thinking about this as some spaghetti dripped off his chin and onto his plate. He looked a little doped by the way Leila saw it. As always she teased him about it. "Hey! Cuz! You alright? Hel-lo?" she waved her hand in front of his face for his eyes to blink. Lance suddenly came out of his mini coma and looked at Leila who was frantically waving a fork in his face. He didn't want her to poke him. "Hey, 'Drooling Monster of Despair and Dopiness!' wake up! Haha snap out of it Lance." ranted Leila. As soon as Lance came back to "life", Leila asked the waitress for their check.

Chapter 6

Leila linked her arm with Lance's as they came out of the restaurant. Tickled to the core by his cousin, Lance was grateful that she wouldn't let him pay for their meals. But she still loved him and vice versa. Leila hung on to Lance and he held his arm over hers because he felt a sense of security wash over him, and he felt protective instincts settle in. They walked around some nearby gift shops that were right around the corner of Olive Garden. Cute little souvenir shops and local tourist hotspots were on each side of the tiny village's street. Lance began to feel tired and exhausted from the trip. He decided now really wasn't the time for a little quickie deals at the cozy shops. He stifled a loud, unintentional yawn in front of Leila. Some resting did *he* do while he was on that plane.

Heading back to their vehicle, Lance lazily slid into the passenger's seat allowing Leila to put the car in reverse and head backwards onto the road with another shift of the gear into drive. Lance leaned in his seat far back to rest awhile. He was starting to snooze away, and began to dream. In his dream, he thought of the Colorado scenery—the pastures that ran off for miles on end, with neighbors well off in the distance yet still close-, he thought about the trees, and the wildlife that roamed in the mountainous evergreens. He was even out there in the meadows of it all, sharing it with one person. In his mind that person looked a little wrinkly and blurry. He was squinting to see the small, skinny and delicate frame of her, but she was out of focus; too far out in the distance. Wait a minute though, he knew who it was. It was Grammy. He smiled. Lance strode closer to Grammy feeling as if he needed her warm and soft hugs.

But all of a sudden, that figure didn't look like Grammy at all and that person got closer as their image appeared very clear, and suddenly a hand reached up and slapped him in the face hard! Lance jumped up from his mini nightmare and realized that what had actually made him jump were the sudden brakes Leila had applied to the car, because wildlife had been thoughtful enough to appear on such short notice. She swerved around the slow-moving turtle and accelerated speed. With a deep breath and a shake of his head, Lance recalled the instant dream and recognized the person to be Nancy. This girl was causing him trouble everywhere he went. Leila looked over at Lance who seemed to have had a disappointed look on his face.

"Lance, you ok? You need to let this girl out of your head. Odds are you'll never see her again, and this was just a mistake. So it's a good thing too because then you won't have to worry about her anymore and she won't have to worry about the loser that tried to kiss her," she smiled as she spoke. "I'm just kidding Lance. You're not a loser, but she *is* for not seeing the true you, haha just your lips!" Leila cackled at her continuous jokes. She really did admire Lance and was just giving him a hard time. The whole while, Lance, with his temple resting on his fist, stared at Leila with a mischievous grin and rolled his eyes.

Then she changed the subject completely which finally got Lance's attention enough to have to hear what she had to say. "Grammy's neighbor, Teresa Mendez, is actually one of Grammy's closest friends. They have done a lot since you've been gone, and Teresa has actually helped Grammy out when I couldn't. Teresa is actually the one who gave me the call that Grammy Evelyn is not feeling well. She says she wants to do a special surprise for her. Isn't that sweet?"

At the mention of a special surprise, Lance's eyebrows shot up. "Surprise? Now where did I hear that? Yeah that's very kind of her. How come I never met this lady before? Hmm . . . Grammy has her ways, eh cuz?"

As they were finishing their conversation Leila entered the driveway through the back and parked the car. The place was tidy and clean like Grammy always had it. The log cabin was a dream to live in;

everything Lance always wanted, especially in a home to raise a family in. It had the rich, tan, wooden color to it, and the roof a green metal tint to block the rays of the sun or the powdery snow. The porch was wide enough to throw a party on, and the front side of the house displayed a gray-chalked, rocky chimney. The windows were polished, shiny and majestic. The whole log cabin itself rested on a wide, flat mountainside. The big picture of the beautiful log cabin was absolutely extravagant.

Lance got out of the SUV and pulled out his duffel bag. Leila opened the front door with her key, the sound jangling. The scent of the house reminded Lance of his youthful years as a boy, and how he'd run in with muddy shoes, or come down the steps to the kitchen while Grammy was cooking dinner to finish his homework, or when he and Grammy would just cuddle on the couch with a nice movie playing. The events replayed in his mind as he blinked, breathing in the aroma. He blinked again. His young, boyish self was gone. His Grammy was gone.

He wondered if maybe Nancy would be gone too. He didn't want to know. Leila flicked the lights on of the living room. Cozy as it seemed, Lance retrieved his bag and headed upstairs to his old room. Leila went into the laundry room to feed the dogs who'd been barking after they heard the footsteps of the squeaky stairs. There were two dogs; Minnie was the toy terrier and Brutus was the German shepherd. Although it seemed like an unlikely pair, they were two great buds. Lance could hear Leila sweet talking them as he unpacked his things on his bed.

"Oh hey baby doll!!" she squealed. "Oh yes you are! . . . Yes you are! Hey buddy, how are you pal? Ahh! Don't jump on me! Bad boy! Down. Good boy! Here's a snack guys . . ." Leila said the whole time in her high pitched voice. Lance chuckled as he could just picture Leila with her funny looking faces. She was probably flashing them a clown smile right now. Then he thought about the dogs. He could see tiny Minnie resembling Nancy; small, fragile . . . yet cute and himself as Brutus; tough, big, and protective, not to mention good-looking!

Lance thought he could use a shower before hitting the sack, and so he prepared his things for the tub. Lance entered the welcoming bathroom that Grammy always kept nice and tidy and smelling nice. He set his things on the rack inside the shower. He needed his masculine soap, his refreshing shampoo and conditioner, and his foot scrubber to keep his feet from stinking up a whole place. Lance turned the faucet on and immediately hot water gushed out. He unplugged the drain and closed the curtain as he undressed for a nice, relaxing shower. Lance looked into the mirror that began to fog up, but he noticed himself looking empty and feeling sad. He couldn't explain it, but there was something that bothered him so much. Was it the chance that he missed by skipping the job interview; the opportunity to finally achieve his dreams, the possibility to finally become what he'd been waiting for his entire life? Was it his Grammy; the one person who could understand him, the true human-being that never gave up on him, and the precious heaven-sent-angel whom was really sick in these moments? Was it Nancy; the girl whom could let Lance be himself around her, an honest girl with a kind heart, the woman Lance actually thought could potentially be "the One"? He didn't know!

He hopped into the sizzling water to help relax his tensed, muscular body. He knew he would ease a bit of pressure from his long, steamy shower. Lance grabbed his masculine scented soap, and scrubbed from way down to the toes and upwards towards his abs and biceps, then continued to his shoulders and to his neck, finishing off with a nice cleansing of his distinct jawline, his cheekbones, and his forehead. He rinsed off his unsettling, unimaginable day, and clasped his skillful hands over his face to wash off the remaining soap; then he breathed a sigh.

Taking the shampoo off the rack, he squirted it out onto his palm and ruffled it onto his scalp full of dark brown hair. He lifted his chin up to the hot water and let it hit his face. Then he washed off the shampoo, and ran a hand through his hair. Lance was beginning to feel at ease with himself. With his eyes still closed from shampooing, he lifted the sides of his lips into a full grin. He was here for Grammy, the love of his life.

With that thought in his mind he turned off the faucet and grabbed his towel hanging on the towel rack. He dabbed it in his face and dried all the millions of water droplets that left him to be wet. Opening the shower curtain, he felt surrounded by all the foggy, steam as if he were in a sauna. He dressed into comfortable, snug sweat pants and a shirt that fit snug to his body as well, showing off his ripped out body even for sleep! He brushed his teeth to be squeaky clean and shiny to prepare himself to light up Grammy's hospital room early in the morning.

Quickly, he went downstairs to grab a bottle of water and say goodnight to Leila. They would talk more in the morning, but now he wanted some rest. Heading back up the steps, he stopped short as he spotted a picture frame sitting on a shelf on the wall of his Grammy and himself. This was going to be tough if he found out something bad would go down, especially anything that affected her, because not only would it get to him, but also tear Lance to pieces.

Back in his old room, he laid down in his bed full of sheets that held all sorts of modes of transportation-trains, cars, and boats. He remembered that he didn't get those because he had a thing for automobiles or vehicles, but because of his love of traveling and going to different places that he decided he wanted those specific decorative sheets. His Grammy hadn't changed a thing in there. He rested his head on his arms and looked up at the ceiling. Man . . . what a day. Although he loved traveling, getting some sleep was the next thing on his list. Lance turned his head to the window and looked out. He saw lights on at the neighbor's house. "Must be Mrs. Teresa," thought Lance, and he closed his eyes.

However, he immediately opened them again when he saw a slender figure with long black locks, move to a dresser, stand there, and appear to probably be looking at a mirror. Could that be? No . . . Was it her? He wasn't sure, but he was determined to find out in the morning daylight. His heart began to accelerate, its already pounding self. In all his adult years, he never ever felt this strongly for a woman whom he just met. Crazy, insane, or whatever the heck he was, he knew that he wouldn't let her get away this time.

Chapter 7

Bright light allowed Lance's sleepy eyes to slowly open up, as he realized the beautiful morning sun was shining up a new day that showed promise, and a whole bunch of surprises. Leila was obviously skilled in her cooking because an amazing smell arose from the kitchen, up the stairs, through the door of his bedroom, and up into Lance's nostrils. He rubbed his face while he sat on the edge of his bed. He had a lot to do today he thought as he got up and headed for a man's cave called the bathroom.

Later he dressed, and skipped a million steps to the bottom to eat a wonderful breakfast. Leila, as usual, was her bright, perky self and had a nice smile to go with it. Lance rested his arms on the square counter in the center of the kitchen, grinning. Leila held a pot in her hand and turned around beaming her bubbly personality. She glided over to Lance and kissed him on the cheek. "Good morning, Lance. Did you sleep well?" she asked.

"I slept like a rock. Um, hey Leila when did you say we would see Teresa Mendez? I want to know this 'angel from heaven'," he said as he used the quotation-mark signal. Leila stared at Lance with a mild grin. She poured her cousin a bowl of nice, sweet oatmeal and a grapefruit, and 2 waffles drizzled with syrupy goodness. She knew he had a big stomach. Serving his plate at the dining table, Leila proceeded to tell Lance the plans for the day.

"So, I was thinking we go over to Teresa Mendez quickly before we leave to see Grammy at the hospital, just to let her know where we'll be. We'll also drop off those set of Christmas lights so she can use them for her surprise," she pointed to a box dull of clear and colored lights sitting on the floor next to the laundry room where the dogs were. "She is the sweetest lady I met next to Grammy! Plus she has family over. A very nice woman. We should get her a pie or something after we visit Grammy, don't you think?"

Lance, gobbling his meal up with a bit of syrup dripping from the side of his chin, nodded in agreement and said, "I think we could get her some flowers too. Do you know who is with her, exactly . . . erm," he managed.

Leila looked suspiciously at him. Knowing her cousin too well, she knew he had something up his sleeve. Or was about to. She put all the dirty pots and plates into the sink to wash them later. She stayed silent for a moment to let the pause set onto Lance's skin. "Hmmmm . . . maybe, maybe not. It depends," she said leaning her back towards the sink and crossing her arms to her chest. "Why is it so important to you? What are you going to do Lance?" she asked.

Lance took a gulp of his mango juice that he had always loved as a kid, and only the little town of Pagosa Springs sold it at the market place as a substitute for orange juice. Grammy always served it to him, and now Leila had done the same, only she was pressuring him into spilling the beans about his plan. Although he had no idea if the woman he saw last night was even Nancy. Aha! So he was still thinking about her! Why? His conscience tugged at him.

"Alright! I just thought that maybe Nancy would be there. Just a gut feeling cuz, nothing much. Are we gonna leave now? I know it's stupid, but I just have to find my soul mate," he said as he pressed his hands onto his heart with a girlish smile on the last sentence. He winked at Leila and went to the dogs to feed them their breakfast.

Minnie and Brutus were hopping up with joy each happy to see him. He went into the room and grabbed the snack treats for both dogs. He patted Brutus on the head and scratched under his chin; Brutus thumped his back left paw on the floor, enjoying the goodness of the relievable petting. Then he picked up tiny Mini and petted her soft, furry head. They are so adorable he thought. "Alright kiddos, your breakfast is served. Enjoy your meal," said Lance leaving the doorway.

Leila grabbed her purse and the keys of her car. She wrapped her scarf around her neck in one swift motion and headed out the door. Lance hoisted up the box of lights and followed out the door. Leila drove the car into the neighbor's home a few 800 meters along the road. Then, turning onto the dirt road leading to Teresa Mendez's home, was a beautiful log cabin. It was behind a little lake in front of the house, and it displayed amazing glass windows that showed off the inside of the home. The morning sun shone off the water's surface showing little gleaming, sparkling dots of light on every single wave that flowed up and down with the wind's easy breeze.

Parking in their long driveway, Lance felt a pounding in his heart though he didn't know why. Ok maybe he did, but he didn't want it to lead in a wrong direction. He wanted her to feel the same feelings for him as well. Who was he kidding? He had really no clue as to if Nancy was truly there or not. For all he knew, the woman he saw last night through his bedroom window could have been Teresa Mendez. But for some reason his heart continued to pull in the direction of hope and fulfillment; he knew that had to be . . . . Nancy.

Getting out for a brief moment, Lance and Leila walked to the front door to the Mendez's home with Lance carrying the box of Christmas lights. Leila knocked on the door and waited for a few minutes before a middle aged woman with hair tied up in a bun, opened the door with a welcoming smile. She was about 5"5', and she had a pretty slim figure, and she had nice eyes. Her creamy skin color seemed familiar and her nose resembled that of Nancy, but it could have been a coincidence. The nice woman was indeed Teresa Mendez and she spoke with a kind heart saying, "Why hello! I'm so happy to finally meet you, Lance. I've heard so much from your beautiful Grandmother! Would you care to come in to get fully acquainted?" she asked tugging Lance inside her home.

Leila giggled, as she countered her offer by saying, "Oh no Teresa, thank you. But we were planning on seeing Grammy first. Um . . . but we also came quickly to let you know, and drop off this box lights you asked me for. Is it okay if we come back later?" Teresa nodded with every statement she said. "Sure, sure! Here let me take those," she said as she continued, "I have a wonderful idea! Why don't you come over for dinner tonight? It'll be splendid, and you can meet my family, and we can get to know each other . . ." she jabbered on. Lance chuckled and put his hands in his pockets. "That'll be great Mrs. Mendez," he said, but was surprised when she cried, "Oh please call me Teresa! That makes me sound old! We're all friends here!" she smiled. They agreed to meet her back later and stay for dinner, then left to the car, and Leila drove off.

Chapter 8

"She's in room 102," said the nurse at the front desk. Leila and Lance gave a polite nod to the nurse and slowly turned the corner through the hall to Grammy's room. Lance reached the room first and stared at the room door, before entering. He thought about how she might look, if she was asleep, if she would know what was going on. He didn't want to think so much about it though. His heart pounded in his chest and his pulse accelerated. He took a deep breath and Leila waited patiently behind him squeezing his shoulder with a supportive hand.

Opening the door, Lance quietly stepped in. There she was, his Grammy, wrapped in hospital blankets instead of her own homemade quilts. There she was, eyes closed for sleeping instead of praying. There she was, sick, pale, and weak instead of healthy, alive, and strong. He choked back a soft sob. He put his fist to his mouth and pressed it as he tried to compose himself. A huge knot formed in his throat, but he tried not to let it affect him. He stepped closer towards Grammy's bed until he was right at the edge of it.

He looked at her lovingly, at her dark brown hair beginning to slightly turn gray. Her pointy nose held the oxygen mask inside her nostrils for air. The monitor connected to the IV in her wrinkly skin showed her heart rate. It was steady, calm even for someone whose heart rate almost reached 160mm. It seemed as if she knew Lance was there. He was her baby from the very beginning. She sensed his presence and it made Lance almost breakdown just realizing it.

Lance bent down and kissed her forehead, which was warm and soft. He caressed her head with his hand and then picked up her hand. He held it in his, and gripped it. Leila who had been watching the whole thing with tears in her eyes came over to Lance and Grammy. She put a hand over both of theirs and leaned in to kiss her beautiful grandmother. Lance made a silent prayer to the heavens above and hoped that God received it like a mailed letter.

Suddenly, a stir of movement arose from Grammy's body. Her neck moved softly from side to side. It looked as if she were getting herself comfortable. She then opened one eye; then the other. Lance made a quiet gasp. His Grammy knew he was there; her son had come to visit her. Moving her head towards Leila and Lance, Grammy looked peacefully at her adopted children.

Lance felt his heart jolt and leap out of his chest. He immediately leaned in close to his Grammy still grasping her soft, delicate hands with his. Her eyes twinkled at the sight of her boy and he felt the connection that foretold the hugs and kisses shared, the support amidst him in every way and most importantly her love of which signified their unity forever even after one of them was gone; but he couldn't think about her leaving him. He couldn't thin of her breaking a part of his heart. And he certainly couldn't think of her passing away without staying a while longer and her witnessing him and a family of his own. He needed her to hold on and stay; his adopted mother, no his true mother, had to be there . . . just had to.

With so much of her strength already gone, Grammy mustered up a few words to her grandchildren. "My Darlings, I am so glad you came. I missed you both. I need both of you to know something though. Please don't feel any anguish, but if I am not well by the time you need to leave, please . . . I give the house to you my dear Lance. And to you sweet Leila, my car. My money goes to equal share for both of you and—" she was cut off by Lance who would not hear the rest of her statement without her knowing how he felt.

"Shh sh sh shh . . . Grammy, save your breath, please. You will listen to *me* right now."

"But Lance . . . let Grammy finish, she may have a point," countered Leila.

"No Leila! She needs to hear *me* out first. Grammy you will not leave us no matter what you say. Your stuff is still your stuff. You will not go anywhere, and I will not leave you until I know you are 110% well. If it takes me 5 years then so be it, heck if it takes me my lifetime I don't care!! But I won't leave your side Grammy and you for sure won't leave mine. We love you, *I* love you . . ." his voice cracked at the meaningfulness behind his last words to her. He choked back the soft sobs he had been holding the whole entire time he was in that room. Then, he just couldn't take it and had to leave the room for some privacy. He gave her a kiss on the forehead, and left his Grammy, each of them containing tears in their eyes.

He strode to the door of the room, and without another word left. He squeezed his eyes shut while pressing his fingers to them. He went to press the elevators button to go down to the ground and out of the hospital, out of all the sickness and sadness, out of the burdens that chained him so tightly. He just couldn't take it anymore. He needed some time for himself to think about his thoughts that gnawed at him. He needed some time alone so he could wrap his mind around reality and escape the fairytale he so wanted to come true. With the elevator taking the lifetime his grandmother needed, he decided to take the stairs all the way down.

He pushed open the balky door open with some ease. It seemed that his pressure level of temperament was a little high, and he could do almost anything. He skipped about a hundred steps and flew across to the hospital's exit. He was finally outside! He felt the chains and the tight ropes around his neck and body dissipate and Lance took the deepest breath of air he could manage. His whole body felt so weak suddenly that he crouched over and supported his hands on his knees, as if he had just finished a marathon and couldn't get a grip on himself.

He walked over to a nearby bench and plopped himself down. Lance knew he didn't want to continue thinking about the condition his Grammy was in or where he was at the moment. The first person that popped into his mind was Nancy. Could she be the answers to all his prayers? But wait . . . the thing is he hadn't been praying. He had been so busy lately that he hadn't stopped and thought about the most important person who could actually solve his problems. God was there the whole time and Lance ignored his presence. Lance had been too busy to realize he didn't stop and talk to God, his Savior.

See the thing was that Leila, who had become this way with Grammy's help, shared more about God each and every day to Lance that finally deciding to visit the nearest Adventist church, he believed he made a right decision. Lance got involved in the church as much as he possibly could. He grew spiritually intimate with God that there was such a strong bond, Lance even had faith; he got baptized. But then as he studied for exams and classes, he wound up a little tangled, heck a little more than tangled. He lost the chemistry between God and himself that he no longer desired to pray or visit the church. He was a total dropout. He really needed to ask for forgiveness.

He gave no attention to the One who had been blessing him and making him His top priority. Lance felt so ashamed and stupid. But he was so blessed that as a child Grammy, being so faithful in her religion, had also shared with Lance the love of God and took him to church with him every Saturday. It seemed like Lance wiped it all away with the rain in this moment in his life right now as well.

He knew he had to make this right with the Creator before he messed things up for sure. He knew what he was about to ask God, so in the middle of the hospital's sidewalk, he knelt down to pray to the Lord. "Lord Jesus, my King and Savior . . . my heart, soul, and mind are all weak. They are weak in You, in Grammy, in myself . . . Lord I know I have messed up, big time, but I ask that You may replenish the holes in me and help me to get up from the path I am walking; the wrong path. Lord I can't fight these battles without You, and I know I've been trying to do it myself . . . I need You. Please forgive me, help me to be strong and wise in these hard times. Please, bless Nancy, wherever she may be, and that You may also guide her in the right path, so please protect her as well. I ask that you take Your Mighty, healing hands and wrap Grammy in Your comforting arms. Please stay with Leila who has been here through thick and thin, for she may need you as well. Thank you for bringing all these people in my life, and for surrounding us with Your love even though we may not deserve it, but You are a God of Love, Power, and Strength. Thank you once again Lord, and in Jesus' name I pray, Amen," he finished his prayers with gleaming little specks of water droplets, slowly sliding with serenity. Suddenly, a sense of tranquility washed over him and filled his whole body, making him feel at ease. Lance knew God was in control.

Chapter 9

On the way back, Leila calmly patted Lance's shoulder as *he* was the one driving now. Leila had always been supportive; it was one of her big qualities that defined her character. She took a deep breath and turned her head towards her window. They returned back to Grammy's lovely home, and quickly got out. They were going to change for the dinner they would be having at Teresa Mendez's home.

Leila went to go shower as Lance comforted himself on the living room sofa. It was leathery, soft, and so inviting to sit on. The dogs came to him both and he picked Minnie and placed her on the couch next to him. She rolled over as that was always her favorite thing to do when she knew a good belly rub was coming. Brutus laid his head on Lance's leg and Lance patted him. He scratched Brutus behind the ears and under his chin. Brutus' left leg began to thump loudly on the floor. Laughter rumbled out his throat as he saw this tiny twitch from both dogs. Leila came out of the shower and Lance hopped himself up. Heading to his room to get his personal stuff Lance asked what time they would go?

"6:50! And its 6:25! So get busy!! Oh and Lance, please be on your best behavior," she yelled at first and then calmly said as she came closer to Lance. Lance shook his head and closed the door of the bathroom. He took a heavenly shower and freshened himself up. He gelled his hair, applied his cologne, brushed his teeth, and put on his leather jacket. He felt good, ready, prepared for anything that were to come to him tonight. He wanted to enjoy himself whether Nancy was there, or not.

They got to the bumpy road entrance of the Mendez's home. It looked exquisite in the moonlight, and all the lights around it twinkled like a star. It looked beautiful off the water's reflection. The inside seemed like artifacts in a museum encased in a glass b0x. Heading to the door; Lance felt a little skip of his heart jump up and down. He gulped his saliva down and rang the doorbell. Leila clung to his arm as he rubbed his hands together in the chilly night. Then the wonderful woman who greeted them the first time appeared at the door.

"Lance! Leila! How very good to see you again. Welcome! Come in, make yourselves comfortable. Feel right at home, please," said Teresa in a delighted voice. She guided them to the living room where she allowed them to sit down. Lance took the invitation and sat down politely nodding his head in gratefulness to be in the presence of lovely people. Once seated, Lance took a moment to look at everything around him.

It was one heck of a home! It displayed the beautiful light wooden logs all over the house. The steps were smooth, sliced logs lining all the way upstairs. The chimney had a rock wall that went vertically on one side of the house, and the floor looked shiny and slick. The furniture fit perfectly like a puzzle piece to a jigsaw puzzle. The sofas were leathery brown and complimented the room well with its beautiful features, while the rugs on the floor matched everything. The entire home was amazing. He wished he had a home like this . . . and a family to go with it.

Before he could daydream any further, a voice interrupted his thoughts. "Lance darling, I'd like you to meet my niece who is joining us and visiting me. I know it seems like you can't believe it, but I am in fact an aunt," she giggled. Her eyes squinted as she smiled a pretty smile. Lance looked amusedly at her and said, "Of course, I'd love to Teresa," he grinned. She smiled happily at him and called her family. They might have seemed to be in a different room, a play room maybe? Lance looked at Leila who was also waiting for the family to be greeted.

"*Mamita,* come here! Evelyn's grandchildren are here! And get your *Tio* too because our guests are here," yelled Teresa at her family with a Spanish accent. Lance wondered where she could be from. He liked getting to know different cultures and people from other descendants. She had Latin to her, a sort of spice that just naturally came out from her. He was interested in that and would ask her later when they ate. Where were these people? He was starved!

"I'm coming! I'm coming! I didn't know what shoes to wear, and can you tell me where I put that *blusa? No la encuentro.* I can't find it. *Tio's* closing the window upstairs and—," said the niece who raced down the steps and didn't care to look up until she reached the bottom step stopping midsentence from her Spanglish speaking right in front of them. Lance looked wide eyed at the lady. The lady looked wide eyed back at Lance. Leila and Teresa both looked from one another to the two oglers. Something fishy was going on and the apparent awkwardness seemed to drift around the room. Lance finally broke the ice and said, "Nancy."

Chapter 10

Teresa Mendez's eyebrow shot up. "You know each other?" she said shocked, as was Nancy who had her mouth open slightly and her eyes glared at Lance with a little timidity. She seemed as if she saw a ghost and the present seemed to swallow her whole back to the horrible past that seemed to lurk with details for the future. "*Mamita* answer me! What is it? Have you met before?" asked the anxious Teresa. Nancy swallowed, took a deep breath, and shook her head out of her hypnosis.

"I uh . . . we uh . . . he picked up my book at the airport. That's all. And it's nice to see you again," she said forcing a smile. It was Leila's turn to twitch her eyebrow up. She smirked at the situation unfolding in front of her. And to turn down the heat she spoke saying, "Hi. I'm Leila, Lance's cousin. I know we have *not* met. It's nice to meet you." She extended her hand out to shake Nancy's with a smile. Nancy now mixed up looked from Lance to Leila and to her Aunt. She licked her lips and sucked in her breath. Finally deciding to speak she burst the air within her out from her body and said, "Wait a minute, hold up. You're telling me you are related? You both aren't a couple? I thought that you guys were—"

She did not finish her sentence for Teresa broke in saying, "Nancy no! They are *both* the grandchildren of Evelyn. Now please go get your grandfather to begin dinner for the evening." Lance looked at Nancy with a look of hurt in his eyes. There was so much plead and want that surged throughout his body, and it was slightly apparent that Nancy was the reason for all of it. With a turn of her body, Nancy retrieved upstairs to fetch her uncle.

Once downstairs, the group sat quietly at the table. Teresa asked Lance if he'd be willing to pray, and to Nancy's surprise, he agreed. They each grabbed each other's hands, and bowed their heads. "Dear Lord, our Almighty God," he began with Teresa approving it with a loud 'Amen', "Thank you kindly for the friends my Grandmother Evelyn has. Thank you for allowing Leila and I to join these people, these wonderful angels from heaven to dine with them and eat a wonderful meal." Nancy still listening to the prayer looked up at Lance who was so enclosed in the prayer she thought the Holy Spirit might choke her for her being so unkind with him since he had arrived. Continuing he said, "Bless each person here; Teresa, Mr. Mendez, Leila, Nancy . . . , and myself. But Lord, please be especially with a very important person in my life," with that Nancy remembering those words when they sat next to each other in the airplane shot her head up, but listened as he was about to say who it was. ". . . the person who has been with me only all my life. A beautiful, loving, admirable woman, and also an angel from heaven, my grandmother; Grammy Evelyn. Thank you Lord . . . Amen."

As Lance finished his prayer, Leila, who had been sitting next to him, squeezed his hand. She knew it had been hard for Lance to hear the words about their grandmother being sick. In her mind, she just wished things would get better and that Lance would be alright; she hated seeing him this way especially when there were two women involved. And this night when she got the chance, she would make sure to have a word with Nancy and let her know what the situation was with Lance and that she should consider giving him another chance. Speaking of Nancy, she seemed to have eased a bit about Lance, and she even looked heart melted in a way right after the prayer.

Nancy felt horrible inside. She had assumed the wrong things about Lance. It was wrong that she thought about him having a girlfriend when it was really his grandmother, and it was wrong of her to call the security patrol on board of the airplane when he hadn't really attacked her. It was a kiss for crying out loud, and who couldn't deny that she just as bad wanted that kiss? It's just that maybe it was too soon? No! When they sat down to speak, it felt as if they had known each other for years. She was going insane at the moment and needed to take a chill pill. She didn't know how the events of the night would play out but she knew in her heart, deep down, she was going to talk to him, and for all she knew, he wanted to talk with her.

Luis Mendez looked at Lance and said in a NewYorican accent, "Lance buddy, you know you can call me Luis. Not many people call me 'Mr. Mendez' you know. You know something? You look like an athlete. What do you do? Cause' you know, I use to play a little bit of eh sports myself." He nodded his head as he waited for Lance to reply with enthusiasm. Lance swallowed his first bite of the Latin dish of rice and beans with a side of *vianda* that contains: yams, plantain, potatoes, cassava, and a mixture of onions and a certain type of fish called *bacalao*.

He answered Luis," Alright Luis, whatever you say. And of course I play sports. I love basketball and baseball, they are my favorite sports. I do a lot of exercise when I can. I go to the gym often and some side sports such as volleyball and running. Plus I know how to ski and snowboard too. Shall I say more . . . ? Haha I guess it's safe to say I'm an athlete."

"I know one thing you're not good at . . . ," mumbled Nancy, "respect of personal boundaries." Lance and Louis who both grinned at each other looked over to Nancy who had intentionally replied her hasty comment. Four pairs of eyes stared at her with indignation; one of which she knew were most offended. Discomfort from all sides of the room, once again, arose in the area. Suddenly to break the tension, Teresa stood and asked if anyone would care to help her prepare the dessert. Lance looked away from Nancy to Teresa. He smiled at her and nodded in agreement. While they left, Leila asked if she and Nancy could speak a minute alone.

Nancy took a deep breath and with little encouragement agreed. She usually wasn't like this. She was full of a bubbly personality and eagerness overflowed her. She guessed it might have had something to do with her unappreciated remarks regarding Lance and how low centered she'd become since his arrival. As she thought about this, Leila directed her to the back porch patio with a heating radiator on because it was still a brisk night.

Leila turned to Nancy and got straight to the point. "You know, Lance isn't the bad guy you've portrayed him to be or else I wouldn't be asking you right now to give him another chance. I have no idea what went on that day you two met, but I can assure you that if he didn't do what he did then it wouldn't have meant that you mean so much to him. Ever since that moment, he realized that maybe the person to fill him up completely could be you, because you began mending his battered heart. All he's ever spoken about is you and that he has to find you or else without you he'd just give up . . .

Listen, Nancy you might think I'm intruding in your business, but Lance . . . he's my cousin and he's family; one of the only people left in my life. I don't want to see him wounded any further. So please do me a favor and don't judge him by what you don't know about him, because I guarantee you'll learn something new that you didn't expect. He's never felt this strongly about anyone and even if you both barely know each other Lance is willing to do just about anything to be near you. I mean come on! Did you see the way he looked at you in there? He's basically asking you to see him through only this time without slapping him, please," Leila smiled at the last part.

Nancy stared guiltily at Leila. She felt a pang of her heart when Leila spoke all those details about Lance to her. She knew it was wrong of her to assume the negative about him and pretend he was just another ordinary guy. But the thing was that he wasn't just some ordinary guy, he was different. All Lance had was "extraordinary" bursting within him. Nancy felt deep within her that Lance was more than she saw him out to be; that he somehow found a way, unknowingly, to tangle the strands of her heart with his and jumble it into a knot. For some reason she felt there was just no way of undoing it.

Leila looked at Nancy's various expressions as she thought. Leila waved her hand in front of Nancy's

face to break her free from the hypnosis. With that
Nancy snapped out of her intent focus and looked
at Leila straight in the face. "I know I've messed
up, but—," she didn't finish because at that moment
Lance creaked open the back porch's door only to
say, "Hey ladies . . . the dessert's ready." He motions
with his head to come in. Leila smiles and says, "Well
actually Lance, I think Nancy wanted to speak to
you. I'll enjoy that nice apple pie, thanks." With that
she walks inside and Lance surprised closes the door
carefully behind her.

He pops his eyebrow up as to wait for Nancy to
speak. She clears her throat as she prepares to say
something without making a mistake. "Um . . . well,
I uh . . . Lance," she looks directly at him with an
expression of culpability. She just couldn't get the
words out. Lance took over, and moved closer to her.
She began to feel the flutter of butterflies in the pit
of her stomach. Her breathing accelerated and she
gulped down the nerve to say anything that might've
made things worse. He inched his way to leave a
minimum of 3 inches between them. Nancy looked up
at the tall, handsome, hunk.

She seemed to feel an urge to tip-toe and kiss him,
because that's what he seemed like he was doing (for
the second time!). But then he pulled out a soft, wool
blanket and wrapped it around her shoulders and he
took a step back. She looked confused once again

and brought herself back to reality. He asked, "Are you okay?" as if she were some little girl with some serious issues.

"You weren't . . . I thought . . . Never mind. Listen, Lance," stuttered Nancy.

"No, Nancy . . . you listen. I know what I did was not right from my part, and that neither of us appreciated the outcome, that's for sure. But I've wanted to search for you . . . to make sure you were alright from that day. I'm truly sorry, and I'll let you be. I just needed someone, besides my Grammy, the most important person in my life," said Lance keenly. He heard Nancy echo 'the most important person in your life' as if she hadn't heard it the first time.

"I thought you meant your girlfriend, and that's why I . . . pushed you aside. Lance I assumed too quickly about you and only thought about myself. I should be the one apologizing for my behavior. You didn't deserve that and yet, you didn't respond harshly. I am . . . Lance, I am sorry. I hope it's not too late for starting all over," she responded. They both knew that in each of their hearts they wanted to begin anew, but neither of them was sure if the other would go along with it. Lance was sure she was just saying that to be nice. He wouldn't have a chance with her. On the other hand, Nancy hoped he would see she was all for another opportunity with him. She really wanted to get to know him the right way without assuming anything from the get-go.

Would they both know the truth about their deep affection for each other? They didn't know. Lance didn't want to be hurt again, but Nancy wanted to work things out . . . how could this be?

Chapter 11

The Mendez's and the Marshall's finished the night with the sound of relaxing Latin music in the background of the peaceful home. After the talk with Lance and Nancy, all five of them moved into the living room for some "family-fun" time, as Teresa put it. Teresa being the one with the whole idea brought a few games out for an interesting challenge before the evening ended. They played a card game, a drawing game, a couple board games, and even a game of charades. Teresa laid out snacks and Louis made his famous hot cocoa for everyone to enjoy. They separated into teams, played every man for themselves, and even rivaled family vs. family.

Lance had stole a few glances at Nancy when she wasn't watching and wondered how he would be able to move on with his life if this true beauty wasn't by his side. He watched her smile, heard her laugh, and he marveled at the way her eyes sparkled; everything about her seemed just right, but if not being with her made her happy, he would learn to live with that. As for Nancy, she couldn't help but bite her lip which curved into a smile every time she looked towards Lance's way. There was no possible way she could give him up so easily without allowing him to redeem him-self to her. Every single quality he possessed seemed to push forward with every minute that to pass by. Although he seeped with care, and kindness she knew he needed her, and for her sake, she needed him too.

Leila stifled a long and loud yawn indicating that she was tired. Everyone knew the night was ending. Lance got up from his comfy spot on the floor, and said," I believe we've all had an interesting evening with so many surprises, but I think it's time for us to go now. We will be happy to stop by again tomorrow for that lovely surprise you have planned for Grammy. Everything was great Teresa and thanks Louis for a fine chat. It was . . . good to see you, Nancy, really good. Let's go Leila."

They all got up and went to the door, Teresa handing them their jacket and coat. Louis slightly hugged Leila and shook Lance's hand pretty rough. Teresa hugged them both with a warm bear hug! Nancy leaned in to hug Leila who then walked out the door. And then, finally it was Lance's turn. They both stared into each other's eyes deeply, and walked in to embrace one another. Lance pulled her in close and breathed in her heavenly, wavy, black hair. Her strong Vanilla shampooey scent invaded the premises of Lance's nose. Nancy squeezed Lance back, feeling his hard ripped muscles on his back. Once again, the connection was there.

Leila waited in the car, the wipers moving back and forth; it had begun to rain while they were there. Lance quickly jogged to the car and hopped into the driver's seat. He put the car in reverse, and as he backed up Lance glanced one last time at the wonderful home, and saw that there, at the window was Nancy with a blanket wrapped around her shoulders, patiently observing him as if she didn't want him to go. And in his mind, he didn't.

Heading home, Leila looked over to him and smiled an odd smile. She herself was just full of surprises and Lance felt the urge to ask, "What?!" His eyebrow cocked up in question from his mysterious cousin. "Oh Lance! You and Nancy will certainly be an item. I can just feel it. I'm telling you Lance, that's your soul mate right there!" Leila seemed so enthusiastic about it. Lance heaved a sigh.

"Sure Leila, sure. I don't think so though. She wants nothing to do with me. How am I supposed to win her heart if she's set the tone? I'm not gonna put myself out there to that gorgeous woman if she doesn't want to know me at all," said Lance. He wished she could see him through all the way, not just piece by piece. Nancy with Lance seemed like a slim chance to him, if any at all. He needed some rest to sleep on the long hard day that had passed before him.

Arriving home at Grammy's, Lance and Leila went their separate ways to go to bed. Once in his old room, Lance knelt down to pray. He knew what he wanted and he knew it would only be what God wanted, but if it were God's will, then so be it. He slipped into his warm bed and slowly as the minutes of the night progressed, Lance fell asleep.

Chapter 12

"Lance! Wake up! It's Grammy! C'mon we gotta go!" startled Leila to Lance. Lance's eyes perked open in an instant, and he hopped out of bed immediately, quickly grabbing his jacket and his shoes. No questions were asked as they zipped their way to the car and out of the driveway and onto the long stretch of road ahead of them. Leila dialed Teresa's number onto her cell and asked if she could feed the dogs for them while they were on an emergency to the hospital. Teresa with her helpful spirit agreed in less than the time it took to even answer.

They sped all the way down to the hospital where Grammy Evelyn was admitted; Lance dropped Leila off at the entrance as he zoomed to an open parking spot and dashed inside behind Leila. They rode up the elevator to her room and right when they got there, it seemed that the surgeon had to perform right in her room because it would be too late if they moved her to the OR. The nurse nearby stopped Lance and Leila from entering the room, who both were watching the doctor slice her up. The nurse pushed them both aside as they began to panic and intrude the premises.

Leila couldn't take any of the chaos anymore so she nearly collapsed, but her cousin held her tight and tears poured out her eyes as she broke down. Lance led her to the lobby's waiting room and sat her down with his arm around her. Lance let her cry on his shoulder. Leila sobbed her eyes out all over his shirt, and Lance caressed her hair shushing her quietly the whole time. As she began to calm, the doctors in the room had not finished, but had stabilized the patient, and wheeled her bed out the doorway, and into the Operating Room.

Leila winced at the sight of it and inhaled deeply the emotions that grasped hold of her neck. The elevators ding sounded in the waiting room with an abnormal tone to it, and Lance and Leila glanced up at the sight of Teresa and Luis walking towards them with 2 plates of food. For a second, Lance's spirits lifted, but then they drifted slowly down when he saw no sign of Nancy. 'I knew it,' he thought. She was no one to count on. Teresa looked worried and displayed a look of empathy. Luis showed no signs of anything, but was somewhat quiet.

"We brought you two some homemade breakfast if you don't mind. I knew you would need the energy," said Teresa smiling politely. "There are scrambled eggs, veggie bacon and veggie sausage, and some slices of bread. I also made you some lunch, but Nancy went to go get that. She'll be here in an hour or so, if that's ok with you. She needed to prepare her photography gear at the moment to be ready for that special surprise, remember? She'll be the one to take some pictures of you, or as she would say, do the "photo shoot" for you guys for Evelyn. The dogs are both fed by the way, Luis did that. But did you get any word from the doctor? How is she? What's happening?" asked Teresa in so many questions.

"*Mamita* hold it! So many questions for them right now. You're probably, how you say . . . , overwhelming them too much! Give them a break, don't you see they need it?" countered Luis to Teresa's banter. He put a hand to her arm as to stop her from her overload of questions and statements. He knew his wife could get carried away at times. He offered a thin line of a smile and apologized for his wife's behavior.

Leila's petite face displayed tracks of the tears shed from a little earlier, but her mood began to lighten up just a little bit and she managed a short smile. Lance looked at his troubled cousin and remembered for a short second when they were younger how when she cried, she would come to him for comfort, and looking at her now he could see her 7 year old self all over again. He squeezed her in a mild hug. Then he replied back to the married couple. "Teresa, Luis . . . Thank you both for the breakfast, and thank you for feeding the dogs and also for showing up here without needing to. When we got here they were just beginning to operate on Grammy, but the nurse pushed us aside from seeing anything although we did see quite a bit. No doctor has attended us from that moment. We have no clue what's going on or what's happened, so . . . anyways you don't have to stay."

"Nonsense *papito*, we will stay as long as it takes and as long as we need to. Alright? Don't push me aside Lance, I'm here for you. So are Luis and Nancy; you can trust us. You know your Grammy is really a special person ok? Why don't you both eat your breakfast first though? Then when Nancy comes to bring you your lunch, if you guys are up to it, maybe you can do the special surprise for Evelyn. It's up to you guys though."

Lance was so glad to have more people he could trust, and it all started out with God. He made a silent prayer thanking him. He thought about maybe taking a little time off to go out and do this surprise thing for his Grammy that Teresa talked so much about. He liked the idea of doing it around Nancy too. Plus he didn't want Leila's mind so caught up in Grammy Evelyn's situation; she needed a break too. They all needed to shatter the stress that was taking hold of them. He slowly nodded at Teresa.

Suddenly Luis got a call and turned his attention to the cell phone buzzing in his shirt pocket. "Eh . . . Ello?" he began without sounding the letter

H in the greeting," Aha . . . Ju need me now? Hey I don't know man, I'm kinda busy. Can't you get Miguel to do it? Are ju kidding me? Alright, alright calm down . . . jes I'll go! Wait for me though, don't start. Ok . . . yea bye." Luis hung up the phone and began to speak with a look of fluster on his face. "Uhh . . . I just got a call from the company, and uhh it looks like they need my help. *Mamita* we gonna have to go now. Lance, Leila so sorry to leave so soon. Let's go Teresa. Adios," said Luis with a handshake and hug from both Lance and Leila. Teresa's smile disappeared, and gave an expression of dismay. She hugged both Lance and Leila very tight, and grabbed hold of Luis's hand. They walked off to the elevator and as soon as the door opened they stepped in, leaving Leila and Lance alone . . . once again.

Chapter 13

"Marshall Family?" asked the doctor who had worked on Grammy in the operating room. Leila, who was resting her head on Lance's shoulder, and Lance, who was flipping through a boring magazine left by the hospital, both looked up immediately. They each stood up and walked a few steps towards the doctor's direction. "Yes doctor?" asked Leila a little timidly. The doctor took his time to explain everything thoroughly to the cousins. It was already the middle of the day and they waited long enough, so it was about time they needed these answers.

"It also seems like the surgery helped a lot but she's going to need a bunch of rest. We'll keep her overnight one more day and after that, she's free to go home. But we want to make sure that she'll be in good hands because if any of these preliminaries aren't reached, then any number of consequences could occur. She could damage her heart more than necessary, her breathing could become insufficient, and worst-case scenario she could potentially . . . die. I'm just letting you know what could happen, all right? I can tell she's very special, and she needs to be cared for okay?" the doctor spoke earnestly to both of them. "But for now . . . she's going to be fine."

The doctor patted their shoulders and gave them a meaningful smile.

They each were tender to all the doctor was sharing with them, but when he said that last part it was Lance's turn to begin to tear up. He quickly put his fingers to his eyes to try and prevent any tears from spilling out. His throat began to choke up and his breathing began to get heavier. Leila held on to his waist as they embraced in a side hug. But then he felt another hand, slender and warm, on his shoulder and he knew it wasn't Leila's or the doctor's. It was Nancy's.

The doctor gave them a little time and Leila said," Thanks Dr. Hunt. We appreciate it." She said these words while letting go of Lance simultaneously shaking the doctor's hands. With that Doctor Hunt turned and retreated, a small smile still on his lips. Lance turned to Nancy who had then in the instant put both hands on his shoulder. Lance uncovered his eyes and rested his forehead on her shoulder. They hugged for quite a while and Lance felt, although wanting to cry his heart out but restrained quite a bit from doing so, a huge burden was lifted off. With Nancy there it just made things so much better. He hadn't even asked her to come or be there with a shoulder to cry on, literally; all that happened was so right and he imagined more times like this even though he knew he shouldn't have.

Nancy rubbed his back with words of condolences to the poor 28 year old. In the whole embrace that Lance knew he didn't want to let go of, he could smell her vanilla shampoo again and loved the touch of her silky skin connected with his, cheek against cheek. Leila hugged herself as she watched the two hug each other. Lance snuffled a sigh and then quietly spoke to Nancy," Thank you . . . Thank you so much. Please . . . don't let go . . . please. I need you." Nancy hearing these words felt a trillion skips of her heart deep within her chest. She wondered if he felt it, but she didn't want to let go either, instead wished the moment could last a lifetime. When she thought about a lifetime with Lance she imagined herself being so happy.

How could she think like that so fast? Was he truly a masterpiece of a man, where every detail that belonged to him was the exact proportion to the man she was interested in and perhaps looking for? Except there was no need to look any further; he was right there clinging to her, asking her to never let go. Did he mean for that instant, or for an eternity? All she wanted as she continued to think thoroughly was that maybe Lance was the man for her. She really needed another opportunity with him. "Lance. Everything will be alright now. It's ok sweetie. I'm here, I'm here . . ." said Nancy but then in a smaller voice said, "I need you too . . ."

Lance finally looked up from the long relieving hug, and stared deeply into Nancy's beautiful eyes. She stared back at him very intently. At that moment Leila was no longer there and instead had gone to the restroom to fix herself up. Each took a deep breath. This woman was helping him cope, and he just adored her. If she was here at this moment, could it be that it meant God planned for her to be there? To be in his life? He so hoped with all his heart. He really couldn't let her go. But then his tummy grumbled like a wildfire that needed to devour a forest to be satisfied.

"Aha . . . Nancy, I uh actually need something from you," said Lance a little childish. Nancy looked up at him puzzled. He chuckled and winked at her with a grin, "My lunch." She giggled and turned away from the lingering hug to fetch his homemade Latino meal. She handed it to him, as well as to Leila who appeared right on time. They hugged Nancy in gratitude for bringing the meal, except out of sheer innocence, Lance accidently popped her a quick peck on the cheek. Nancy a little stunned, but at the same time pleased, touched her cheek lightly and looked back at Lance. He didn't seem to notice his mistake as he immediately bit into the deliciously, sizzled chicken breast that was tenderly prepared. Instead she just grinned looking away as she thought maybe he was the Mr. Right she was searching for.

Chapter 14

Lance and Leila were getting ready for the special surprise. They were dressing up for the photo shoot. Teresa had planned for Nancy to snap pictures of the two cousins based on an old time photo she found in a box of pictures that Evelyn had. Nancy showed the picture of little Leila and little Lance together so they would know the project they're going to be a part of. Leila and Lance got excited about the whole idea and some of the pressure from Grammy's situation's released. Nancy smiles as Lance and Leila act cooky around each other.

She positions them to how they were posed in the old crumbly photograph. In the old photo, Lance was dressed in checkered shorts and a green shirt, and he was sitting in a tire swing that was held on by a long thick rope tied to a sturdy, big branch. Leila wore a white shirt underneath a pair of overalls, and had a wide grin that illuminated her whole face. Her hair was divided into two uneven pigtails that were placed on both sides of her small head. She was standing in front of the tree next to Lance who was shining a smile from ear to ear. The sun in the background of the photo was beginning to settle down with a beautiful effect to the picture.

As they continued to goof off, Nancy was testing the focus and details of her camera, so she snapped a few snapshots of the two delighted cousins. Then she said," Alright, alright! I'm ready you two! Stop fooling around, get in position." The two of them giggled, snickered, snorted and everything in between, then they got into the way they had in the old time photo. Lance squeezed himself through the old tire swing that Nancy had propped up for the scene to do the photo shoot with. Leila fumbled with her hands as if she held a toy because that's what she did in the 20 year old photo. The sun was just the perfect setting and almost ready to go to sleep. "Say cheese!" said Nancy for their cue.

They both smiled bright, their squinted eyes directly looking at the camera like little children do. *Click, click* went the camera a ba-jillion times. Then Nancy stood from her stooped position and quickly observed the photo on her digital professional camera and she compared it to the timeworn photo. Perfect, she thought. She really hoped Evelyn would like it. She glanced at Lance who was being pushed by Leila in the tire swing. Amused, she decided that it wasn't time to end the photo shoot.

Chapter 15

It's dark by the time they arrive back home. Leila decided to go home and check on the dogs, plus she was feeling worn out from the day. Lance was happy that the photography session cheered her up; he made a mental note to thank Nancy later. Lance helped Nancy with the boxes filled of photography props and parts of her sets. She led him inside carefully directing him through the obstacles that were laid out all over the place. He was guided all the way up to her room, and he set the box down gently next to her dresser. Lance gave a sigh of relief from letting go of the heavy box and took a moment to observe his surroundings.

Nancy's room looked peaceful and comfortable. He liked the innocent green color that reflected off her walls, and he admired the way her queen bed looked; very elegant with its hand-full of pillows fitted nicely in a perfect order. What he loved the most was that on one wall of the room was a large mirror that all around the edges displayed a number of pictures and photos that were out of order, but almost looked like a collage. These pictures defined her, her personality . . . her life. He couldn't stop himself but he was seriously like seriously beginning to seriously fall in love with this girl. No this woman, named Nancy.

He looked in her direction with a look of love in his eyes, but he soon tried to stop it because he knew she wouldn't appreciate it. Except when he looked her way she didn't seem to push those feelings aside. Instead she extracted looks of compassion, adoration, and something more he couldn't put his finger on. Lance hoped with all his heart that that extra emotion running through her, the foundation to what was causing her to look at him in a powerful way, would be love. Nancy stood upright after leaning from the doorway, and stepped towards Lance's direction.

"Lance. I don't know what it is, but I haven't been able to maintain my focus anywhere, except for on you. I wonder every day how it is that you control so much of me, even when you aren't around. I realize that it's because something strong has grabbed a hold of me and now I can't break free, but at the same time I don't want to," said Nancy gently as she continued to step slowly forward. Lance blinked a few times as if he hadn't heard right. Was she about to tell him that she . . . loved him? Oh Lord, please! Lance's heart skipped a beat.

She came up close to him now inches away. Nancy looked deeply into his eyes, and Lance took it all in. He marveled at her as he tried to stabilize his unsteady breathing. Their heads started to attract

like magnets with strong forces. Nancy's lips parted
for just a half second before they heard the front
door open and Teresa's voice greet with a loud "I'm
home!" Both Lance and Nancy shook from their
absorbed selves and each stepped back. Nancy's
eyes closed as she realized the extreme moment now
crashing down to the floor. Great . . . how would this
moment ever come?

Lance rubbed his forehead with his fingers and
tried to imagine what it would have felt like if this
moment would have not been interrupted. He cleared
his throat and tried to not make what was once a
magical moment into an awkward one. Lance clapped
his hands and said with a half-smile," Well Nancy
thanks for everything, but I gotta get going." She
returned the half-smile and followed him out of her
room and down the steps all the way to the front door.
Teresa was in the kitchen putting away the loads of
grocery that she had gotten from the market in Pagosa
Springs. She looked up from surprise at Lance being
there and said, "Oh! Lance honey, I didn't expect to
see you here! How'd the photo session go, everything
good? Do you need something sweet heart?"

Lance smiled at his heartwarming neighbor and
replied," No, no Teresa everything's great. Grammy
comes home tomorrow. So that's good. Uhh do
you need any help with the rest of your stuff?"
Lance motioned with his hands to the opened door

where they could clearly see the trunk still open with remaining groceries. Teresa's eyes widened and her face expressed a look of recollection as she piped up with a gasp and said, "Lance! Thank you! That reminds me! I was fixing to call Leila so she could explain about the welcoming party for your Grandmother, but now that you're here, I'll just tell you."

Before she told him, she called Nancy to help with the groceries, and all three of them finished putting up the supplies in her Latin disguised kitchen. Teresa invited him to sit on the coach so they would be comfortable as she described the event she happily planned. Lance listened intently as she told how they would put up streamers at Grammy's home, put up a WELCOME HOME GRAMMY EVELYN banner, and of how Teresa would prepare the meal, along with Nancy, Lance, and Leila presenting the special surprise picture album, with the timeworn photo on the front.

Lance felt a sudden relief of his heart and he smiled. He knew he could count on this family. God had a few missing angels up in heaven because he felt with all his might that they were right there, amongst him. He hugged Teresa tightly and gave her a kiss on the cheek. She turned a little red with surprise and touched the spot where he had kissed her. She smiled with gratitude of the gesture. Nancy watched Lance, viewing every detail there was to see and focused on learning it. She saw how his expression turned like a little boy in a candy store when her aunt explained the event of his Grammy's welcoming. She adored him and there was no way out of that. Somehow the knots of her heart sorted themselves out and arranged themselves to be connected with his making her literally fall in love with Lance Marshall.

That night, Lance knelt down to pray. He thanked God he was blessed, because he knew he was. Grammy was coming home tomorrow and there was no telling how everything would go, but he was sure that things would begin to restore themselves in the right order. Nancy especially was the one for him. He truly loved her and he was going to sort out that situation with her, because he believed they would be sticking around each other for more time than he could imagine.

Chapter 16

Lance opened up the car door for Grammy, and lifted her into her wheelchair. She was going to need it before she could walk again, because the surgery allowed her to be in therapy for her recovery. They drove into Teresa's home right on time, although Grammy didn't know what for. She was sure to be surprised. Lance guided her to the door and opened it. Wheeling her in, someone flipped on the lights and the small group of friends yelled "**Surprise!!**"

Grammy gasped with absolute surprise and grinned wide. Her eyes twinkled up like bright stars on a dark night. The whole Mendez family was there, Luis, Teresa and Nancy; Leila of course and some of Grammys good friends from the small village, Pagosa Springs of Colorado. The banner rested on the railing that led upstairs, while streamers of bright festive colors hung around the home. The home smelled delicious, and Lance couldn't contain his growling stomach any longer. While Grammy's wheelchair stood still and everyone came to greet her with hugs and kisses, Lance slipped quietly over to the table that held all the appetizers and he snacked away at the crackers with cheese bites, the chips and salsa, and the tiny club sandwiches with hot-dog spread; specialty of Teresa. His world came together with satisfaction at the multiple munches and crunches of his delightful bites. What Lance didn't notice was how everyone had finished saying hello to Grammy and they were now staring at him with amusement and laughter in their eyes.

Grammy Evelyn covered her lips with the touch of two fingers and chuckled when she knew how mischievous Lance could be. Lance swallowed his bite of appetizers and opened his eyes to the view of everyone else staring right at him, even Nancy. His eyes shot up with a little shock and embarrassment and suddenly the whole place burst out with laughter. From giggles to blasts of cheerful laughs, the home was filled with joy. Then Leila stepped forward to hug him, with the cute sweater she wore. She snickered tenderly and placed her arms around his waist, for that was as far as she could reach. Teresa came up next to sugar him up with harmless kisses, especially for indulging in her Latin appetizers. He enjoyed the attention and was glad to see his beautiful Guardian Angel happy.

But what surprised him was that he suddenly stood face to face with Nancy. She had kept a long stride toward him while maintaining eye contact. Lance gulped with anxiety as she stepped in his direction. The whole room suddenly had a calmer effect. She looked gorgeous in her loose red velvety ruffled blouse, and her tight black skinny jeans with ankle boots, the ones he remembered she wore the first day they met. Her hair was let down in the beautiful, bouncy curls that defined her beauty. Her violet green eyes pierced at him with not regret or hate but actual wholeheartedness. What was happening?

"How should I start? Lance getting to know you, I'd have to say, has been a major rollercoaster, top to bottom. I'm constantly thinking about you, and it's not because of your gorgeous good looks, but it's because you've changed me. And I know, and you know, and everyone in this room knows that there is certainly a strong connection between us. We have a bond, no doubt. So with that being said, can you tell me how am I going to stay away from someone I know I love? Because Lance Marshall, I love you," were Nancy's words as she let go of what she thought was a major speech to the president. Her heart skipped with radiance. She was glad she got that off her chest, because she felt she would explode.

He grinned with a sense of love, but was soon met with soft, moist lips when he realized that Nancy plunged one on him. Taken aback, he returned the warm delicious, kiss and pulled her close wrapping her delicate body in his arms. Everyone cheered, including Grammy, Leila, and the Mendez couple. The kiss was more than he could imagine, but he cherished every moment of it, because this moment

was special. He was excited that there would be
more to come, but first he wanted to respond to her
mini speech saying, "So I assume there are no hard
feelings, considering that whack you gave me the first
day we met?" chuckled Lance. Nancy's eyes sparkled.
"Nancy Mendez, I love you too," he finished and
leaned right back in for another juicy smooch with the
girl of his dreams.

Epilogue

After the celebration of Grammy Evelyn's return, she began to go to therapy for her recovery. With the help of everyone who went to her surprise party, she gained support and became very happy. Her heart stabilized immediately as if there was no sign of any ill condition that might have caused her serious high blood pressure. She and loved ones praised God for that miracle. She cherished the album given to her by Lance and Leila, her two darling children.

Lance and Nancy went out to several dates and each time they spent more time together, the more their love grew for one another. After several months, it was time for Lance to move back to Illinois to apply for a CSI job at a different place. Unfortunately, none were open for hiring, and the time went by where he had time for workouts, hanging out with his old buddies, and lots of time to think; times where usually he would have been up for it, but he really cared more now about having a job! One day though, he got a call from Leila who said there was a job offer down in Durango, Colorado, a 45minute drive from Pagosa Springs and yet just what he had been looking for. Interested and tired of being so far away from his family and friends he decided that he'd move in with Grammy for a couple of months until he could arrange for his own home.

However while having so much time to think, he visited a diamond jewelry store, later to purchase a perfect diamond cut shape ring for the woman he would propose to, Nancy Mendez. Although it was a bit much out of his pocket, he didn't mind if he knew that for the rest of his life the most valuable part was spending his lifetime with Nancy and that was priceless. Excited he called his Grammy and told her he was sure she was the one. Grammy called Teresa who planned a barbeque steak-out at Teresa's home as soon as Lance returned. The day he arrived Leila picked him up, and Nancy had no clue only to be ecstatic that her boyfriend was coming back.

Luis barbecued chicken kabobs for the whole night on the starlit patio and Teresa made those delicious hot-dog spread with bread sandwiches. Grammy Evelyn thought it'd be a cute idea if the main refreshments served would be mango juice, Lance's favorite. Leila was in charge of being the designated photographer since she knew Nancy wouldn't be able to do it. The Latin music was loud and it brought a good vibe with it. The friends and family danced, chatted, and ate while Lance prepared for the highlight of the evening. His heart pounded for the right reason. Nancy Mendez was his love.

In the middle of the event, when nothing seemed obvious and everyone had gathered inside from the patio, Lance asked Nancy to get him a napkin for his face for the barbeque he had smeared on his chin while eating the fresh grilled chicken kabob. Nancy giggled and replied saying, "Oh sure babe." He quickly pulled out another napkin and wiped his face before she could hand him the napkin she'd retrieved for him. Right when she stepped in front of him, Lance gently knelt down. He basically knew she needed the napkin herself because she was going to get emotional. The room got quiet as everyone realized what was happening. Many "Aww's" and "Ohh's" filtered the silence of the excited room. Nancy's eyes and practically every female's eyes in the room watered. She gasped lightly and covered her mouth with both hands. With the most sincere and honest words, Lance began his endearing speech, "Nancy Mendez . . . I have never in my life met a woman quite like you. A woman whom I can be myself around. A woman whose family I have come to love. A woman who has taken my heart. I want to spend the rest of my entire life with you. I want you to be my lawfully wedded wife. Nancy, I love you with all my heart, and it would make me the happiest man alive if *you* could be Mrs. Marshall." Nancy touched her heart with both hands, but Lance took them into his own hands and finally posed the question, "Nancy, will you marry me?" Without a second thought she leapt into his arms, kissing him all over. Everyone there clapped and applauded and jumped for joy up and down. Every single person there were so happy for the bride and groom to be.

Later that year, a couple weeks later, Lance got together with his soon to be boss and began his dream job as a CSI. After finding his stable job, and finally having time to prepare for the wedding, the day before, Grammy and Lance had a special talk. Grammy seemed to have had contacted Lance's biological mother to let her know her only son was finally getting married. Only Lance didn't know that that wasn't the only time Grammy had contacted her. Over the years when he was innocent enough to think his mother didn't want him, Grammy called, emailed, and notified all the details of Lance's childhood to her. Grammy Evelyn kindheartedly explained the details of his real mother's disappearance. Norma, his mother, was protecting him by leaving him with the only person she trusted Grammy, and going to find another state where she could make sure they wouldn't find her baby. "They" as in the people who murdered his father, who was actually really ecstatic to hear he would be having a son with his sweetheart. His father worked with the bank and by being honest, Lance's father Eugene was killed. The robbers vowed to kill any family members left, and luckily all were arrested a few years later. But Norma didn't have the guts to take back her son knowing he would be afflicted with the odd matter. So she left him to stay and live his perfect little life with Grammy. Norma always asked Grammy to allow her to stay connected with her biological son, by showing her pictures, telling her stories, and always sending crafts he made that were directed to Grammy. Norma always wished she could attend or participate beside her son and his life. However, she knew in her mind she had done the right thing, to keep her son alive, but in her heart she had always yearned for those beautiful, tender moments with her son; moments that he had grown with Grammy instead of her. It was for the best though, and she knew it.

Lance felt a tug at his heart, almost as if the missing piece to his heart was stitched back together and mended. Lance didn't become conscious that he had been tearing up during his Grammy's explanations. He quickly gave a mental prayer to his wonderful Savior. Grammy wrapped her arms around her son, and told him to give Norma a chance. He was finally willing to give that opportunity. Lance thanked his lovely Grandmother, gave her a kiss, and hugged her goodnight once more for always watching over him. She truly did work like an angel. They each went to bed to get ready for the next day, the wedding day!

The wedding day was a beautiful ceremony. The setting took place on a flat hill before the beach where grassy knoll meets sandy beaches. The decorations were autumn colored with beautiful white lawn chairs with light brown ribbons tied to the backs of them. There was the arc of where it had pretty white lights hanging down to the floor, and where the priest stood waiting to marry the enchanting couple. The sunset was just beginning to set and everyone got to their places to begin the wedding. Nancy never looked more gorgeous than when she was wearing a neck wrap-around dress showing the back, and a caramel satin bow tied behind. The dressed flowed beautifully, capturing the essence of her petite figure.

Grammy Evelyn was able to slowly walk down the aisle alongside Lance where she kissed him and sat down at the end of it. Leila wore a slimming, sparkly dress that was also a neck wrap-around with her dark silky hair softly curled and pinned with a beautiful coral colored bow and was placed as a side pony-tail; she served as the only bridesmaid to walk down before the bride. The ring was actually given to two special guests to carry down the aisle and they were Minnie and Brutus. Minnie wore a cute look alike bridal gown although it was short, and a tiny veil over her mini head. Brutus wore a groom's vest with a red rose in the little pocket and he held the pillow with the rings pinned into the pillow so they wouldn't fall out. Everyone gasped with joy when they saw the dogs who symbolized the bride and groom to be.

As Nancy walked down the aisle, the wedding march playing in the background, Lance's jaw dropped once again remembering back from the first day he saw her. Their eyes met with the still strong sparkles in them and they both giggled. Nancy's uncle, Luis, walked her down and gave her a kiss before releasing her to Lance. Lance reached out and grasped hold of her soft, small hands. He was just moments away from calling her his wife. "You may kiss the bride" was the next thing they heard after reciting their vows, placing the rings on each other's fingers, and then saying 'I do's'. Lance and Nancy kissed passionately, knowing that this relationship would only get stronger. They separated and smiled for the camera's instantaneous flashes. They were finally husband and wife; combined forces united.

Lance was met with a soft hand to his back at the reception party when the father-daughter dance was going on. He swiftly turned around to see a mildly wrinkled woman with soft bags underneath her eyes, but a lovely smile that resembled that of Lance's. It was Norma, his mother. He didn't know what pushed him to do it, but immediately he pulled her in for a strong hug which was exchanged. They both choked back sobs, because there was certainly a huge bond between them, although Lance barely knew her. He was apparently experienced in that field. After the song ended and Lance had already danced with his beautiful wife Nancy, so he pulled his sweet mother

Norma and they both danced together to the song "Reunited", even though it was a love song, but they were at a wedding so it made no difference.

Good things started happening soon after the wedding. The honeymoon was lovely at a private island rarely known that had a beautiful beach, delicious cuisine, and fun activities. Returning to their new home they began making plans for a bright future. The first 2 years together had passed for Nancy and Lance who both lived in Pagosa Springs, Colorado. Leila got engaged to a wealthy, genuine, good looking pilot by the name of David Pross. He was so handsome and got along great with the family. He was truly a joy to have around.

Nancy became pregnant and soon had her first child, a baby boy named Damian Eugene Marshall; Damian after Nancy's father, Eugene after Lance's. Grammy was the first person in the family to hold her great-grandson. She fell in love with him too quickly. Nancy the photographer was adding more pictures to Grammy's scrapbook album. She had even captured a perfect picture of Grammy Evelyn holding Damian close to her face with an expression of love. Damian gurgled and giggled with his precious little face. Nancy kept the photo and even had it enlarged placing it right above her fireplace. But soon after, a couple months from the time Damian Eugene was born, Grammy Evelyn quietly passed away in her sleep. Everyone was devastated including her son, Lance. He went to Nancy for comfort, and even his biological mother.

Lance was happy though to know his Grammy had the chance to live to see her great grandchild. The years he'd come to know her, well basically his whole life, Lance greatly thanked God for the major blessing he had put in his path. The day of the funeral, Lance and the family wore white, because it was Lance's request to better remember her by. Everyone began to slowly leave and Nancy while holding their first child said, "Honey, I'll be waiting in the car. Take your time sweetheart. Okay?" she gave him a bear hug along with his mother Norma who was following behind. Lance took a moment to look at the large gravestone which was different than most others. Although it was a bitter moment, he wasn't sad anymore, for he knew she wouldn't want that. He knew she would always be in his heart. And just as it read on the gravestone that resembled that of wings, he knew that God did him a favor by putting in his life his, "Guardian Angel".